**SUPER
HEROES**

BATMAN™

TALES OF THE
BATCAVE

HARLEY QUINN'S
HAT-TRICK

by
MICHAEL DAHL

illustrated by
LUCIANO VECCHIO

Batman created by
BOB KANE WITH BILL FINGER

raintree

Raintree is an imprint of Capstone Global Library Limited, a
company incorporated in England and Wales having its
registered office at 264 Banbury Road, Oxford, OX2 7DY –
Registered company number: 6695582

www.raintree.co.uk
myorders@raintree.co.uk

978 1 4747 5490 3
21 20 19 18 17
10 9 8 7 6 5 4 3 2 1

British Library Cataloguing in Publication Data
A full catalogue record for this book is available from the British Library.

Editor: Christopher Harbo
Designer: Brann Garvey
Printed and bound in India.

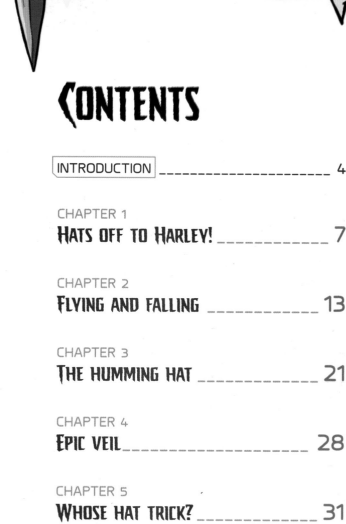

CONTENTS

This is the BATCAVE.

DEADLY GIANT TOP HAT

It is the secret headquarters of Batman and his crime-fighting partner, Robin.

Hundreds of trophies, awards and souvenirs fill the Batcave's hidden rooms. Each one tells a story of danger, villainy and victory.

This is the tale of a deadly giant top hat that is now displayed in the Batcave . . .

CHAPTER 1

HATS OFF TO HARLEY!

Two strange flying objects race above the gleaming buildings of Gotham City.

WHIRA-WHIRA-WHIRA!

One of the objects is the Batcopter. Inside are the famous crime fighters Batman and Robin.

"Over there, Batman!" shouts Robin.

They are chasing a giant, soaring sombrero. And sitting at its controls is the dangerous villain Harley Quinn.

"Give it up, Harley," says Batman.

Harley turns in her seat and laughs at the Caped Crusader.

"I've got hats on the brain these days," she shouts. "Let's see if your brains can handle my straw hats!"

Harley flings several hats into the air behind her. The hats are gold and shiny.

"They're not straw hats. They're SAW hats!" yells Robin.

"Cute, huh?" says Harley Quinn.

BUZZZZ-ZZZZ-ZZZZZ!

The razor-sharp saw hats spin towards the Batcopter.

ZING-G-G! ZING-G-G!

They slice off the tips of the Batcopter's rotor blades. With shorter blades, the copter wobbles off balance.

Batman tumbles from the cockpit.

CHAPTER 2

FLYING AND FALLING

Robin leans out and throws a rope to Batman.

The hero grabs it and swings safely below the Batcopter.

"That's cutting it close," says Batman.

The wobbling copter slows down. Harley Quinn speeds away.

"Hang on, Batman," says the Boy Wonder.

Robin grabs the control stick and pulls
it back.

The Batcopter darts sideways between buildings. But its short blades can't handle the weight of two crime fighters for long.

Soon the two heroes see the flying sombrero circling back.

Harley Quinn has another trick up her sleeve.

She picks up a jester's cap. She points the cap's open end at the Dynamic Duo.

"It's *jester* little something I stole this morning," she shouts.

FWOOOOOSHHH!

Strong winds blow from the jester's cap.

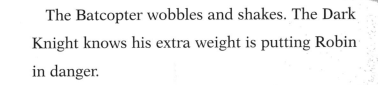

The Batcopter wobbles and shakes. The Dark Knight knows his extra weight is putting Robin in danger.

"Keep after her!" Batman says. He lets go of the rope and leaps towards the buildings below.

"Careful, Caped Crusader," shouts Harley. "Bad stuff can happen at the drop of a hat!"

The Batcopter straightens out. Robin steers away from the stream of wind.

Batman throws a Batarang towards a nearby flagpole. The weapon's rope wraps around the pole and slows his fall.

The hero lands safely on a rooftop.

While Robin chases Harley Quinn by air, Batman follows them below on foot. He leaps from roof to roof.

Soon Batman sees Harley's sombrero swoop towards an old, empty building.

CHAPTER 3

THE HUMMING HAT

A huge billboard displays the building's old name:

WEDDING DAY HAT FACTORY

On top of the building sits a huge bridal veil and a giant, upside-down top hat.

With a leap and a flip, Batman lands on the top hat. He stands and watches Robin flying down to join him.

Suddenly the top hat tilts.

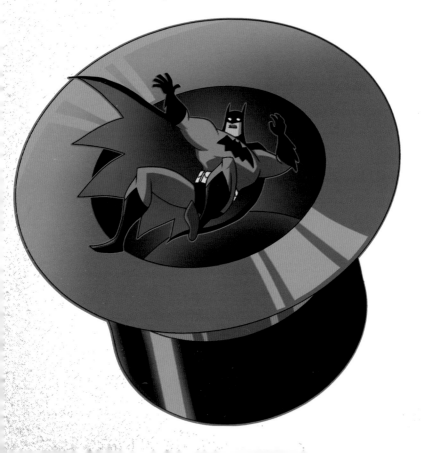

Batman loses his balance and slides into the top hat's giant opening.

The Dark Knight puts his hand against the inside of the hat. It is as smooth as glass.

Harley hovers above the hat in her sombrero.

"You've fallen right into my trap, Caped Crusader," says Harley. She presses a button on a remote control.

HUUUMMMMM!

Batman feels a soft vibration under his boots. He is suddenly pushed against the inside of the hat.

The giant top hat is spinning.

Batman sees his foe flying above the hat.

Harley giggles. "Now I'm off to snare the Boy Wonder. I have a plan that can't *veil* – I mean *fail*!"

The top hat spins faster and faster.

The spinning force crushes Batman against the wall. He knows a Batarang could help him climb out of the hat.

But the force pins his arms flat against the wall. He can't reach his Utility Belt.

Batman presses his palms against the wall. Slowly, he uses his powerful muscles to inch up the side of the hat.

The hat spins faster. It grows harder and harder for him to move.

His head feels dizzy. Batman sees flashing points of light.

He knows this is what people see before they pass out.

CHAPTER 4

EPIC VEIL

The Batcopter swoops towards the rooftop of Harley Quinn's hideout.

"Where's Batman?" Robin demands.

"Oh the Dark Knight isn't feeling well," says Harley. "I believe he caught something that's going around!"

"But I'm glad you came, Boy Wonder,"
continues the villain. "You always say that
crime doesn't pay. Well then get a load of
my *net* worth!"

Harley pushes another button on her remote
control. The giant bridal veil begins to expand.

Suddenly the veil springs towards Robin.

The netting grows wider and wider. It hovers above the Batcopter like a dangerous cloud.

It's too big! thinks Robin. *I'll never get away in time!*

CHAPTER 5

WHOSE HAT TRICK?

A glove reaches out of the top hat's opening.

With his last ounce of strength, Batman pulls himself to safety.

The hat is still spinning. Its motion tosses Batman high into the air.

SWOOOSSSHH!

The hero uses his cape to catch the air like a large kite. Batman coasts down to the factory rooftop.

"Robin!" he calls. The Dark Knight is worried about his partner after what Harley had said.

Batman hears the whir of the Batcopter. He looks up to see Robin aiming the damaged rotor sideways.

The blades blow the giant veil into Harley Quinn. The veil wraps her in its sticky mesh.